Forgotten Girl

Steampunk OZ: Book 1

by Steve DeWinter

Summary

There is no yellow brick road here. No emerald city. No lollipop guild. This is the Australis Penal Colony, a continent sized prison referred to the world over as the Outcast Zone. Built to contain the world's most dangerous criminals, OZ ended up the dumping ground for everything polite society deemed undesirable.

Book 1

From inside OZ a garbled message proves Dorothy's father is still alive, trapped in a prison with only one way in and no way out. Into this place 17-year-old Dorothy must go if she wants to find her father and keep the promise she made to her dying mother.

This book is a work of fiction. References to real people, events, establishments, organization, or locales are intended only to provide a sense of authenticity, and are used fictitiously. All other characters, and all incidents and dialogue, are drawn from the author's imagination and are not to be construed as real.

eBook Edition

ISBN-10: 1-61978-032-1

ISBN-13: 978-1-61978-032-3

Paperback Edition

ISBN-10: 1-61978-033-X

ISBN-13: 978-1-61978-033-0

Chapter 1

Professor Benjamin Gale gazed out the window at the fog. Even without the white mist obscuring everything beyond fifty feet, the island continent to the north was still far enough away, he never would have been able to see the coastline from the smaller island that served as the gateway for every criminal sentenced to the Australis Penal Colony.

His wife, Elizabeth, tugged at the black satin lapels of his wool frock coat and did her best to brush off imaginary specks of dust from his sleeves. Her eyebrows furrowed as she attempted to adjust the folds in his fiery red ascot tie. "I wish you'd wear a color that was a little less showy."

Benjamin flashed the perfect smile he had used to get funding, resources and a personal visit once with Queen Victoria. "I am asking the Council to set aside nearly 15,000 British Pounds from the annual budget for my proposal. I have to stand before them and look like I know what I'm talking about."

She finished fussing with his ascot and looked him in the eyes. "That smile of yours may have won my heart, but the men in there…"

He placed a finger tenderly on her lips. "If I could convince someone like you to marry someone like me, I will not have any trouble convincing a group of pompous old stuffed shirts to fund my project."

Someone cleared their throat behind him.

Benjamin spun around to see Bartholomew Danbury, the youngest member of the Council at 68 years old, frowning at him through a monocle. "My fellow pompous stuffed shirts are ready to see you now Professor Gale." Bartholomew turned away and disappeared through the door.

Elizabeth shook her head. "I'll be waiting in the carriage outside with Dorothy."

He gave her a sheepish grin before he followed Bartholomew.

Bartholomew was only slightly taller than Benjamin, but his height was mostly in his legs and, while he was not walking hurriedly, Benjamin had to jog to catch up with him.

"You know I'm not talking about you, don't you?"

Bartholomew kept to his long stride without slowing down.

"Just be thankful I'm the one who came out to get you."

He did not see how Bartholomew could move so quickly in the heavily starched, fitted frock and waistcoat that had become the most popular attire under Queen Victoria's reign.

He trotted alongside Bartholomew and tried not to sound winded. "So what is the feeling of the room today? Do you think they will set aside the money for my proposal?"

Bartholomew stopped abruptly and Benjamin almost crashed into him.

"We've known each other for a very long time, so I will be frank. I remember when you were just a brash 19-year-old with lofty ideas to convert the southern landmass into the world's largest prison. And you did it. You changed an entire continent into the inescapable Australis Penal Colony. But I think you did too good of a job."

Benjamin laughed and opened his mouth to defend himself.

Bartholomew held up a gloved hand. "It is because of your innovative designs that we have been able to slowly reduce the number of personnel needed to keep the penal colony running and under control. In fact, the Council is considering shifting guard duties to some of the more behaved prisoners; thereby, bringing the non-inmate count in the colony down to zero within a year."

He could not keep his mouth shut after that comment. "That would be a mistake."

"This is not the same prison you and I built twenty years ago, Ben. Times have changed and the recommendations of the Council have to change with them."

Benjamin barked out a mocking laugh and motioned to the inner chamber doors. "One of those changes was to deny all requests for parole. I designed the colony to mimic polite society for purposes of rehabilitation, not containment."

"Take a look at the effect that one change had on the rest of the world. Crime is down 70% all over the world. Everyone, people and nations, are more civilized to each other. Mission accomplished Ben. Accept your pat on the back and take your latest invention to London or New York in the Americas. Let somebody more deserving have first crack at your machine."

Benjamin was shaking his head. "You know what everyone's starting to call the Australis Penal Colony don't you?"

Bartholomew shrugged his shoulders. "People call it many things."

"They're calling it the Outcast Zone. A place to send the undesirables from society and forget about them."

"Maybe it's time you forgot about them too."

He could not believe he was hearing this from the same man who supported him from the very beginning. "Take me before the Council, Bartholomew, before I say something I will regret."

Bartholomew pushed open the doors leading to the Council's inner chambers. "Don't say I didn't warn you."

Benjamin walked into the Council Chambers and paused at the edge of the top of the stairs that led down to the presentation platform. He slipped a small wooden box from the pocket of his frock and gripped it tightly.

He thought about what Bartholomew had said.

His hands sweated around the edges of the box. All he wanted to do was scream at these self-indulgent morons that they were all making the biggest mistake of their lives. They could not, in all conscience, abandon the people in the penal colony.

But that would only get him immediately ejected from the Council Chambers and he would not get a chance to say what he had come to say even if, according to Bartholomew, they weren't going to listen anyway.

He quickly dismissed all negative thoughts from his head. The Council was made up of reasonable men, he assured himself. They would listen to what he had to say.

Then they would do the right thing.

He would outline his proposal and they would see why it was not only the best thing for the penal colony, but for the world. His invention would effectively change the human condition in more ways than one. He had to make them see that, and now he knew exactly what to say.

"Please step forward, Professor Gale." The Council leader's voice echoed loudly in the acoustically designed chamber and startled him. His head snapped up and he had to crane a little higher to look up at Phillip Weston, the Council leader, who sat in the center of five occupied chairs that formed a semi-circle on one side of the room. His friend Bartholomew had already taken his seat on the far left.

He surveyed the construction of the Council Chambers and hated how the members of the Council sat in a raised banister section above the presentation platform in the center of the room. To make matters worse, and to make the Council appear that much more foreboding, he had to walk two more steps to the center of the room where the platform stood raised a foot above the rest of the center of the room with its own little railing for presenters to lean on if they began to feel dizzy as they addressed the Council.

"All the world's a stage," he whispered silently to himself as he mounted the steps and stood on the raised platform. He always thought of that familiar line from England's most famous playwright every time he came before the Council.

He cleared his throat and heard it echo throughout the entire chamber.

Here goes everything, he thought as he stared up at the row of ancient men who stared back down at him.

Outside the New Kansas Council Chambers, the air was not as choked with soot from the countless coal fires as it had been in New York and London. However, a thick blanket of persistent fog had lingered throughout the city for the third day in a row, and the bright blue skies over Dorothy Gale's home in the Americas seemed but a distant memory.

Everything was better back in America. The water was better. The food was better. Even the people behaved better back in America. She had only been here for two months but she was already homesick. And this did not bode well with the reason why she was even here.

Normally her father would make the trip to New Kansas on his own, leaving her and her mother back in America. However, she was nearing her 10th birthday and would no longer be educated by the governess at home. She was finally of the age where she should be sent to a proper school for young ladies.

Their journey together as a family doubled as both a business trip for her father and a school-finding trip for her. As she sat by herself in the carriage parked outside the New Kansas Council Chambers, she plotted how she was going to convince her parents to let her attend the school that was within walking distance of their home.

Even at the tender age of nine and nine-tenths, Dorothy loved her mom and dad and did not want to spend any time away from them if it was not absolutely necessary. And in her mind, being sent to some boarding school in a foreign land was not absolutely necessary.

Her mother exited the front door to the Council Chambers building and headed for the carriage. Dorothy had been unsuccessful in trying to convince her parents to not send her away to school. Every time she talked to them, they would quickly convince each other that it was the best thing for Dorothy to attend one of the top schools in the British Empire.

Maybe a change of tactics was required. She would turn her mother into an ally, and together they would convince her father to let her stay home. That would work, Dorothy thought to herself. Divide and conquer.

"I don't know why I didn't think of this before," she whispered to herself as her mother climbed up into the carriage.

"Were you saying something, Dorothy?"

"I was just wondering how long Daddy would be."

"He just went in to see the Council. It might be a while."

Dorothy smiled. Her head swirled with the many ways she could eloquently tell her mother that the best school for her would be the one that kept her close to her family.

When she had formed the most brilliant sentence in her mind that would convince her mother that keeping the family together was the best option for everyone concerned she opened her mouth and blurted out, "I want to go to the school close to home."

Her mother breathed an audible sigh. "We've gone over this many times before, Dorothy. Your father and I want you to have the best education possible, and we just don't think that the public school near our house can give that to you."

"But it's where all my friends are going to go."

"You'll make new friends."

"I don't want to make new friends. I'm happy with the ones I have!"

This conversation was not going as well as Dorothy had hoped. Even worse, it had spiraled out of control almost immediately.

"We'll discuss this when your father returns."

Having failed so miserably, so quickly, Dorothy wanted to burst into tears right then and there. But she knew her mother was stronger than most and would never allow her to cry.

As she fought back the tears, all Dorothy could do was stare out the carriage window and hope that her father got what he wanted so he would be in a good mood.

The Council leader's voice echoed in the massive room like an exploding cannon as he banged on the gavel to quiet everyone down. "That will be enough Professor Gale!"

Benjamin disagreed that it was enough.

"Don't be stupid enough to think…"

"I said that's enough!" The Council leader punctuated each word with an increasingly harder bang of the gavel until the handle snapped off at his final word.

Benjamin's upper lip quivered. He had not expected to let his emotions get the better of him.

But when the Council announced that this would be their final session before dissolving and letting the penal colony operate on its own without any outside influence, someone hurled vulgar insults at every Council member. He looked around the room to see who had the nerve to say what he was thinking and was shocked to discover that the insults had come from him.

How would Elizabeth recover from this idiotic blunder, he thought and then reminded himself that she never would have made such an idiotic blunder.

His wife would not be happy that he let emotions cloud his judgment. She was always the more logical of the two, which seemed to be the absolute reverse of just about every other couple they knew. They hid it well enough to blend in with Victorian society, but he always felt out of place at the gentleman's club and she was never satisfied with the local ladies sewing circle.

He also reminded himself that, despite the lunacy of their actions, these were still reasonable men. He could appeal to them in a reasonable manner.

He took several deep breaths, looked up at the head of the Council and did his best to replace his quivering lip with the smile that had gotten him this far.

"I sincerely apologize for my outburst Councilman Weston."

"I will not tolerate outbursts of any kind from anyone during my sessions."

"I understand. But about my invention…"

"There is no budget for the Australis Penal Colony, Professor Gale, as there is no longer an active council to oversee the colony."

He lifted the mahogany box in his hands. "If I could just show the Council my…"

Councilman Westin held up a hand to silence him.

"I am sorry Professor, but the rest of this session is devoted to finalizing the closure procedures for this Council and approving the hand off procedures for control of the Australis Penal Colony to the designated inmates. We do not wish to hear any new proposals regarding the colony."

"But I…"

"I suggest you take your ideas to the Royal Society of London. If your device is as crucial to the future of humanity as Councilman Danbury says, the Royal Society is in a better position to listen."

He stood there staring up at the Council, his mouth opening and closing, trying to come up with the words that would make them change their minds. He saw Bartholomew tilt his head and shrug his shoulders in an "I told you so" manner.

"That will be all Professor, you are excused."

"Please stop kicking the seat, Dorothy." Dorothy's mother never looked up from her dog-eared copy of Les Trois Mousquetaires.

"I see you reading that book all the time Mother. Haven't you finished it by now?"

"I have finished The Three Musketeers several times now sweetie."

"You know they've translated that into English. You don't have to read it in French."

Elizabeth folded the book into her lap and smiled at Dorothy. "The English translations edit out some of the better parts of the story."

"What better parts?"

Elizabeth smiled wider. "I'll tell you when you're older."

"Older, older. Always when I'm older. When will I be old enough for anything?"

Elizabeth opened her book and began reading again. "When you're older dear."

Dorothy crossed her arms in defiance and turned to look out the window of the carriage again. She could not see very far.

A thicker blanket of fog, if that was even possible, had rolled in while talking to her mother and she could just make out the front doors to the Council Chambers.

She stared at the doors and willed them to open.

This time they did.

She squinted through the soft haze to see who had just walked out. In the long black wool coats and gray trousers, every man from London to the East India Trading Company looked the same. When a flash of red cut through the fog, as if it were a tightly focused lighthouse, she knew instantly to whom it belonged.

Dorothy shot up from her seat and leaned out the carriage window. "Daddy!"

Her mother grabbed her dress to keep her from toppling out.

"Daddy!"

He squinted back at her through the fog and waved a hand as he hurried over to the carriage. The springs groaned and the carriage rocked as her father climbed into it.

Her mother was the first to speak. "How did it go?"

"They wouldn't even listen to my proposal."

"Well, it's not the end of the world honey," she said.

His face grew somber as he stared into her eyes.

Her face grew just as somber. "Is it?"

He sat back and let out a big sigh. "It was bad enough when they cut the funding for the woodsman project, and let all the security automatons fail one by one, rather than send in repair teams. It was even worse when they rejected my tactical observer proposal. But this time they have gone too far."

Dorothy's mother tried to reassure him. "It can't be that bad."

He looked at her mother with an intensity Dorothy had never seen before. "The Council is gone. They are turning over control of the Australis Penal Colony to the inmates. Nobody on the outside is going to know what's going on in there."

Dorothy could not remember her parents behaving like this. Ever. It sent a sudden shiver down her spine. "Daddy?"

He turned toward her and his face instantly softened. "I'm sorry honey, your mother and I don't mean to frighten you." He looked at her mother and then back to her before reaching into the pocket of his coat. "It's a bit early, but I thought now would be good time to give you your birthday present."

He pulled out the small wooden box from his pocket and smiled at her.

All her fears melted away in an instant. "What is it? What is it?"

He handed her the small box. "Open it and see."

She tilted the lid back on its hinges and stared down at two perfectly shaped emerald hearts. She blinked her eyes a couple of times in surprise. It looked as if they both glowed brightly from an inner light. She looked out the window to see if the sun was reflecting off the emeralds causing them to sparkle, but a dark blanket of fog still enveloped the city. She looked up at her father. His face reflected the green glow coming from both emeralds.

"These two emeralds are special. They generate a form of energy when in close proximity to each other. The closer they are to each other, the brighter they glow."

She reached for one and paused. "Can I touch it?"

"None of the energy is lost to heat."

She gave him a quizzical look.

He laughed. "Yes, Dorothy, you can touch it."

She reached into the box and took one out and held it in the palm of her hand. "I love it."

Her father slid the box back into the pocket of his frock. "As soon as we get home we'll have it mounted in a necklace for you."

Dorothy's mother looked at her father. "I don't remember seeing any jewelry shops here in New Kansas."

"I meant back home, in America."

Dorothy's heart skipped a beat and the edges of her mouth felt like they were going to tear, she was smiling so big.

Her father stared out the carriage window at the Council building. "There's nothing left for us here." His eyes glazed over as he stared through the building and beyond into the impenetrable fog. "There's a storm coming, and the old fools don't even know it."

Dorothy hopped up and down in her seat. "When are we going home?"

Her father smiled at her. "I will book passage on the next ship out of here. Speaking of going home," he said as he glanced up at the ceiling of the carriage. "Why are we just sitting here?"

He banged his hand on the ceiling of the carriage. "Driver."

Dorothy's parents exchanged a look before her father poked his head out the window. "Driver?"

Two strong hands grabbed her father by his wool coat and pulled him out the window and into the street.

Dorothy screamed. Her mother jumped up as a second man appeared at the carriage window and pointed a flintlock pistol at her. "Why don't you two ladies sit for a little while longer?"

Dorothy's mother settled back into her seat. "It's okay Dorothy, everything will be all right."

The man smiled, most of his teeth decayed down to the swollen gum line. "That's right missy. Everything will be all right as long as you stay quiet."

Dorothy's mother winked at her before turning to the man with the gun.

"With how moist the air is with all this fog, I doubt your flintlock will even spark."

The man's rotting grin gaped wider. "Are you willing to stake your life on it?"

He shifted the muzzle of the gun and pointed it at Dorothy. "How about the life of little girly here?"

Outside, her father struggled with the man who pulled him out of the carriage. There was a sudden noise, as if somebody hit a hollow log with a stick, followed by a grunt, and then everything went quiet.

The man with the rotting teeth laughed and stepped back from the window. "You two stay put if you ever want to see him alive again."

She had not realized she had been holding her breath until she heard her mother exhale.

They both watched as the second man grabbed her father's limp legs and, with the help of his bigger associate, carried him off into the fog.

As soon as the men disappeared around the corner, Dorothy's mother yanked a Derringer double-barreled pocket pistol out of her purse. "Stay here Dorothy."

The carriage rocked violently as Dorothy's mother leapt to the street and ran to the corner of the building.

She took a quick peek around the corner and then pressed herself flat against the wall. She looked back at Dorothy and mouthed "stay put" before she raised her Derringer with one hand and gathered up the folds of her skirt, exposing her legs in a very unladylike manner, with the other.

She took three quick breaths and disappeared round the corner, her Derringer held out in front of her.

Dorothy held her breath and stared unblinking at the corner of the alleyway, waiting for her mother to come back out with her father. She was just about to jump out of the carriage and follow her when a gunshot tore through the silence and made Dorothy jump.

The fog muffled the sounds, but Dorothy thought she heard someone cry out in pain.

Two more gunshots in rapid succession echoed from the alley.

That was one more shot than her mother's Derringer held. She could not stay in the carriage any longer. She had to do something.

She jumped out and ran across the street before skidding to an abrupt stop along the edge of the building. She was about to run into a gun battle without a gun.

The carriage driver always carried a pistol in the strongbox next to his seat. She could use that one.

She ran back across the street and reached for the handholds on the carriage when she noticed she was still gripping the emerald heart her father had given her in the palm of her hand. She slipped it into the deep pocket of her coat and clambered up onto the carriage where she stifled a scream and froze.

The driver was slumped over in his seat with a pool of crimson red forming all around him.

She gripped the railing and worked her way to the other side of the driver's perch where the strongbox held his pistol. She paused when she saw that his hand had already disengaged the lock but still held on to the latch. The men who attacked had not given him time to do anything else. But how had they managed to kill the driver without anyone noticing? They were sitting in the carriage the entire time and had not heard or felt anything.

She did not have time to worry about that now, her mother needed her help.

Dorothy stared at the hand that held the strongbox closed. His final act of courage had now become a barrier to getting the pistol.

She gritted her teeth as she took the tips of her fingers and clamped them on the driver's hand. Shivers went up and down her spine as she handled the cooling flesh. This was not something a proper 10-year-old girl should be doing. But, getting that pistol was the only way she could think of to help her parents. Without a weapon of her own, she would be completely defenseless. This was her only option.

She peeled the fingers off the lid of the strongbox one by one and let the hand fall limply to the driver's side. It shifted his weight and he fell to the side. That's when she saw the crossbow bolt embedded in his heart. Her stomach churned and threatened to expel what was left of her breakfast. She swallowed a couple of times and forced herself to remain in control.

Her mother had taught her to be strong, and that's what she had to be.

She lifted the lid and scooped out the flintlock pistol.

She quickly checked it and knew enough from watching her father clean and load his guns that this one was loaded and ready to fire.

She was now in a position to help.

And she was going to do whatever it took to help her mother get her father back.

She jumped down from the carriage and ran to the corner. She pressed flat against the wall and peeked into the alley.

There were two bodies lying on the cobblestone pavement in the alley. She immediately recognized one of them. "Mother!"

She ran and skidded on her knees to her mother's side.

"Mother, are you okay?"

Her mother's eyes fluttered open and focused on Dorothy. A small smile creased her lips. She spoke barely above a whisper. "Find your father."

Tears welled up in her eyes. "I won't leave you Mother."

Her mother weakly reached up a hand, her gloves soaked in blood, and brushed a strand of hair from in front of Dorothy's face. "Don't cry sweetie, you have to be strong."

When she spoke, Dorothy could see her mother's teeth rimmed with a red liquid that welled up from her throat. She coughed, sending her into a full body spasm. Dorothy held her head and tried to keep it steady. "Hold on Mother, I'll go get help."

She gripped Dorothy's arm. "Use the emerald. Find your father."

Dorothy shook her head. "I'm not letting you die."

"It's too late for me."

"I can save you. I just have to go get help."

"Save your father, he can save everyone."

"I'm not letting you go."

She smiled at Dorothy through the pain that was clear on her face.

"But I'm letting you go." Her mother closed her eyes and her head lolled to one side.

"Mother?"

There was no response. She shook her gently. "Mother!"

A scuffling sound on the cobblestone made her look up and she saw the man who her mother shot trying to crawl out of the alley.

Dorothy jumped up, grabbing the driver's flintlock pistol, and pointed it at the man.

"Don't move. Or I'll finish what my mother started."

The man rolled over to one side and grinned that hideous rotted smile at her. "Aren't we a feisty one?"

Dorothy's tiny hands barely made it all the way around the wooden handle as she struggled to keep the pistol steady. "You killed my mother."

The man looked past her at the still form of her mother lying in the alleyway behind her and then back up to her. "I guess there's no sense in denying it, is there?"

"Where's my father?"

"I wouldn't know."

She pulled back on the pistol's hammer and took a step closer. "Tell me where he is or I'll..." She let what she hadn't said hang in the air for a moment.

His response was to laugh. "Or you'll do what? Shoot me?"

Her heart pounded deep in her chest, making the pistol tremble even more. It did not escape his attention. He tilted his head to the side. "No. I don't think you'll shoot me."

She gripped the pistol's handle tighter. "Tell me where my father is, or I will."

The man chuckled. "I'm sorry, but your threat is just not as strong as the threat of the man who hired me." He continued to drag himself across the cobblestone, grunting with the effort as he did so.

"I'll shoot you, I really will."

He stopped to catch his breath. "There is an inherent flaw with your threat. You see, if I tell you what I know, the man who hired me will have my family killed. I can accept my own death better than that of my wife and daughter." He looked differently at her this time. She did not like it.

"You're about the same age as my daughter. I'd hate for her to never be given the chance to grow up, fall in love, and have a family of her own. I do not want my daughter suffering for my sins, so I will afford you the same opportunity to not suffer for the sins of your father."

He started up again with his slow trek across the alley.

"What does someone like you know about love?"

"Don't judge me by my outer appearance, or my actions here today."

"Tell me who hired you. The police can put him in jail and your family will be safe."

The man laughed again as he made it to the edge of the alley. He twisted himself around and sat up against a stack of barrels that ran along one edge of the wall. "The man who hired me is already in jail."

"Then what are you afraid of?"

"His reach extends to the four corners of the world. Being in jail has not affected his influence on others at all. In fact, I think he prefers it in there."

"Then you can tell me who he is."

"I'm afraid I can't do that lass. He always covers his tracks." The man swiped his hand against the cobblestone and a flame blossomed at the end of the Lucifer match he held in his fingers. She jumped at the sudden movement and almost squeezed the trigger.

He looked at her over the bright flame of the match. "Run."

He tossed the lit match over his shoulder and into the barrel behind him. Only then did she notice that the barrels stacked three high along the edge of the wall were all marked, in bold black lettering, as "GUNPOWDER".

The world around her slowed to a snail's crawl.

She let the pistol fall from her grip as she turned to run out of the alley.

Behind her, a blinding flash announced the impending arrival of a massive explosion.

The shock wave lifted her off her feet before throwing her back down onto the cobblestone and shoving her out of the alley. The world returned to normal speed as she tumbled uncontrollably across the street.

She stopped face down and watched as bricks rained down all around her. She could not hear the individual bricks crashing back down to the ground over the continual high-pitched wail in her eardrums. When the shower of debris ended, she slowly tested her arms and legs. No broken bones.

She pushed herself up and looked at the massive holes in the sides of the two buildings that used to enclose the alley. The alleyway itself was nothing but a gaping hole in the ground. She stared at the destruction with no idea what to do next.

If there was ever any hope of saving her mother, that was gone now.

And the only person who knew who had taken her father was also gone.

Then she remembered her mother's last words.

Use the emerald her father gave her to find him.

Dorothy's heart raced as she dug into the pocket of her coat and pulled out the emerald heart.

It still glowed, but was much fainter than when the emeralds were next to each other.

That was it! The emerald would glow brighter when she was near him. She could use it like a compass.

She had a way to find her father.

She pictured the layout of the city in her mind's eye and tried to decide which way they traveled when they left the other side of the now destroyed alley.

She closed her eyes and let her mind sweep over the city like a falcon hunting its prey.

Around her, a small crowd had gathered, drawn by the noise of the explosion. People were yelling and screaming through the fog about containing the fire that had erupted in one of the buildings.

Someone touched her shoulder and asked in a soft voice, "Are you okay little girl?"

Her eyes shot open.

They must be headed for the docks.

They were going to take her father off New Kansas on a ship.

She looked up at the woman. "I'm okay now."

She took off at a dead run and flew through the city, heading toward the docks on the east side.

She paused halfway there to catch her breath and looked at the emerald. It had grown fainter.

That's not right, she thought. "It's not getting brighter," she said aloud.

She spun around and looked in the other direction of the city. "Unless, I'm not getting closer."

They must be taking him off the island by a ship. But not a ship made for the ocean. They hadn't headed for the docks. They must have taken him to the airfield.

She spun around and ran as fast as she could back through the city.

She paused once to catch her breath and stare at the emerald. She had to cup her hands to see if there was any light coming from it at all.

When she made it to the airfield, her emerald was completely dark. She ran to the main office and pounded on the door.

A muffled voice from inside replied, "Coming. I said I'm coming."

A man opened the door then looked down at Dorothy. "What do you want?"

Dorothy replied, alternating between speaking and wheezing. "When did the last airship leave?"

"Yesterday afternoon."

"No, no. I mean the one this morning."

"Airships don't depart in this weather."

"It's just fog. I've seen them leave in the fog."

"And above the fog is a storm that's about to break any moment."

Dorothy looked around and saw that several airships tethered to the ground. She looked back at the man. "So, no airships left this morning?"

"I'm a very busy man," he said as he shut the door in her face.

She gulped big breaths of air as she cupped her hands over the emerald.

It was completely dark.

She heard the loud clap of thunder roll out of the sky. With all the fog, she had not noticed the storm moving in. Maybe that's what her father meant when he said a storm was coming.

It did not make any sense. If he had not left by ship, or by airship, how did he get far enough away to make the emerald fade?

She walked around the edge of the airfield office just as the storm above the fog broke and it began to rain.

She leaned against the wall and slid down to sit in the mud that was forming all around her. Her mother was dead and her father was missing. There was nothing she could do about her mother, but there was something she could do about her father.

She looked at the dark emerald heart in the palm of her hand. "I will find you Father, no matter what it takes."

Her mother taught her to have an inner strength that was unshaken by outside events, but today had been too much for her to handle.

All her emotions bubbled up to the surface and Dorothy, still only a 10-year-old girl, could not hold back any longer. She looked up into the darkened sky and let the rain mingle with her forming tears. Together, Dorothy and the world both cried as they had never cried before.

Chapter 2

A solitary airship breached through the storm clouds and into the clear blue sky.

Inside the gondola, Benjamin Gale was shackled to the roof of the main passenger cabin with his wrists raised high above his head. He looked like a ballerina as he danced on the tips of his toes trying to relieve some of the strain his shoulders suffered from having to support all of his weight.

A thin man in an expensive over-frock coat leaned against a table and stared at Benjamin.

The thin man shivered noticeably. "I do wish these gondolas were better insulated, and then I would not need to wear this heavy over-frock. It is most uncomfortable. Are you comfortable Professor Gale?"

"My hands are a little numb, but other than that I'm okay."

The thin man laughed. "Humor in the midst of adversity. An admirable quality Professor."

It was time to get the bottom of this, Benjamin thought. "Where are you taking me? What have you done with my wife and daughter?"

The thin man's face grew somber. "I regret that I am the messenger of bad news."

He struggled against the chains that held his hands. "What have you done to them?"

"I'm afraid we do not bear all the responsibility. Your wife was asked, politely I might add, to wait in the carriage. Instead, she shot one of my men."

Benjamin pulled harder on the chains and tried to get closer to the thin man. "You son of a..."

"Tut-tut Professor; let's leave my mother out of this. We are more civilized than that."

Benjamin strained against the chains that bound him to the roof. "What did you do with my family?"

"Your wife chose her own fate. As for your daughter? She is fast, I'll give her that. We lost her five minutes after the explosion. But not to worry, my men are scouring the city and I guarantee you, before nightfall, she will be safe with us."

"You leave my family alone!"

The thin man walked up to within an inch of his face and stared at him with cold, calculating eyes. "Or you'll what?"

Benjamin felt the shackles cut into his wrists as he struggled to get closer to the thin man. He wanted to inflict pain on this man who killed his wife and was hunting his daughter like a wild animal. If he could just get a little closer, he could bite a big chunk out of his nose.

And then do what, he thought. As long as he was a prisoner of this psychopath, there was little he could do to keep his daughter safe.

They stared unblinking at each other for an interminable minute before there was a faint knock at the door to the cabin.

The thin man snapped out of whatever was going on inside his mind and the features on his face instantly softened. "Are you hungry?"

The thin man clapped his hands loudly and the door to the cabin opened up. A boy dressed in a hooded cloak entered the main cabin carrying a plate with bread and cheese on it. The thin man waved a hand in his direction. "Now here's someone who doesn't need to wear a coat in cold temperatures." He pulled the hood off the boy.

Benjamin's mouth gaped open in surprise.

He had heard about early experimentation using the scientific theory of blended inheritance, where the traits of two disparate male and female species could be passed on to offspring, being tested on humans and other animals. But it was only a hypothetical model, and every attempt to make it a scientific reality always ended in a horrific tragedy. Because of the unpredictable results of early testing on living subjects, practical experimentation with blended inheritance had been banned the world over. Not even scientists who operated far outside the scrutiny of other scientists attempted to continue in this field of study.

The thin man chuckled. "It's not polite to stare Professor."

The boy lowered his cat-like face in shame.

The thin man placed his hand under the boy's chin and lifted his head. "Say hello to the Professor boy. Show him your marvelous teeth."

The boy mumbled something that may have been a 'hello' and looked at the floor again.

The thin man flashed his own perfectly formed and smooth pearly whites in a seemingly friendly and warm smile at Benjamin. "I brought along my employer's little pet to prove to you that we have the scientific capacity to do whatever we want."

Benjamin broke his stare from the half-human half-cat boy and looked at the thin man. "Then what do you need from me?"

"I've already looked over your designs and am impressed by how you plan to harness and focus all the power created by the emeralds into a singular, destructive point. With a little tinkering, I have modified your design into something incredible, but my scientists have been unsuccessful in transitioning it from paper to product. I was hoping you would help me solve my problem."

"If you think I'm going to do anything more for you, you're an idiot. You might as well kill me now."

The thin man laughed. "That is not the only reason you're still alive Professor."

He walked over to the table and picked up the same wooden box Benjamin had shown to his daughter in the carriage. He walked over to him and held the box up. "Alone, each emerald is nothing but a pretty rock. But together these two emeralds generate limitless power."

He lifted the lid so Benjamin could see inside. The box contained one emerald cut into the shape of a heart and a heart-shaped empty space in the crushed velvet next to it. The thin man leaned in close. "Where is the other one?"

The rain suddenly shifted from a heavy downpour into a faint drizzle, but had not completely stopped. It was a rare occasion when more than two days passed without rain in New Kansas.

Dorothy felt like a drowned rat as she sat in two inches of sticky mud. She hadn't moved in over an hour and still leaned against the back wall of the airship landing field's main office.

She cupped her hands and peeked at the emerald. It was still pitch black.

Her tears had dried up long ago.

She looked up at the dark, shrouded sky as the reality of her situation sank in deeper than she sank into the mud.

Her mother was dead.

Her father was missing.

There was no one she knew.

There was nowhere she could go.

She was a 10-year-old girl all alone in a strange land.

She had nothing.

She looked down at the heart-shaped jewel cupped in the palm of her hand.

The only thing she had was the emerald.

But despite her father's promise, even that had failed her.

She could sell it for money and buy a ticket to America.

"No." She said aloud and startled herself.

She couldn't do that.

She slipped the emerald back into the pocket of her coat. She couldn't just sit here. She had to do something.

Her emerald showed her that they did not go to the docks, and the airfield captain informed her that no airships had taken off since yesterday afternoon. That meant her father was still on the island where she could find him.

Every option closed to her except one. She decided to head back to the hotel, collect whatever she could carry, and walk around the entire island of New Kansas until her emerald glowed. She hoped that whoever had taken her father would not get the opportunity to leave the island before she found them.

Dorothy stood up and tried to shake whatever mud she could from the back of her dress. All she ended up doing was caking her hands in even more mud.

Voices shouted in the distance and she looked up to see the cause of the commotion. Several men were jumping out of a carriage.

They were big men. And they were scary looking.

The biggest man, who acted like the leader of these men, shouted orders to the rest. They split up and headed toward different streets. The leader casually glanced around and met Dorothy's eyes from across the airfield. She immediately recognized the big man as the one who pulled her father out of the carriage. He started pointing at her and shouting. The rest of the men all turned and stared at Dorothy.

Her heart pounded faster and adrenaline shot through her veins like a lightning bolt.

Her wool dress and coat were soaked with rain and mud and it felt like she was wearing clothing made out of lead. Her muscles were already tired and, for a fleeting moment, she thought about letting them catch her. At least they would take her to her father.

She quickly banished that thought from her mind. If she were captured too, there was no way for her to rescue her father.

She darted around the corner and into the city. She could hear men shouting from the streets parallel to the one she was on. The weight of her rain and mud soaked clothing was slowing her down and there was no way she would be able to keep running for much longer.

She ducked into an alley and crouched down behind a pile of garbage. She saw a couple of the men run past the alley on either side. Soon the shouting grew quieter as they got farther away from her.

"Hey you! Get away from there!"

Dorothy spun around to see a shopkeeper standing at the back door of his shop. He was carrying a crate of garbage and waved it at her while he yelled. "Go on now! Shoo!"

She stood up and did her best to be polite. "I'm sorry sir. I was just…"

"I won't have no homeless street urchins hanging around my shop. Scares away customers."

She looked down at herself and saw that the explosion had torn her coat, the mud had soiled her dress and the rain had matted her hair. Of course he thought she was homeless. She would have thought she was homeless.

And then it dawned on her. She was homeless. The adrenaline started to break down in her bloodstream and her emotions ran unchecked as tears began to well up in her eyes.

"Oh no. I won't have no sniveling brat hanging around my shop. Go on, get up out of here!"

She walked slowly out of the alley and looked up in surprise when someone yelled out her name. A large man in a dark gray wool coat and black knit cap, who looked like he just stepped off a merchant vessel, ran toward her.

She turned and bolted in the other direction.

"Dorothy wait!"

Now they were calling her by name. It didn't matter, that would not make her stop.

She dashed around the corner and slammed into the back of another man who turned around and looked down at her. He smiled. It was an ugly smile since the man had several teeth missing. "Look who we have here." He grabbed her and lifted her with his big meaty hands.

She struggled, but he held her in an iron grip.

Loud heavy footsteps pounded around the corner and the man in the black knit cap saw them both. He charged forward and slammed a balled fist into the side of Ugly's face.

Ugly took two steps back and dropped Dorothy. She fell to her knees and scrambled to get away from the men as they exchanged blows.

The man in the black knit cap was a whole head shorter than Ugly. But he was fast and ducked out of the way of every swing that Ugly took at him.

Ugly was not so lucky. Every time he took a swing, Knit Cap ducked out of the way and came back to punch him in the ribs. Or on his side. Or on his jaw.

Dorothy was so mesmerized by how Knit Cap dodged every jab and thrust before returning to deal a striking blow on his attacker, she forgot to keep running.

As soon as Ugly went down for the last time, Dorothy remembered she should be trying to escape. Her feet slid on the wet cobblestone as she tried to gain purchase when Knit Cap grabbed the collar of her coat and hauled her into the air.

She struggled against him as he tossed her over his shoulder. "Put me down!"

"Stop fighting!" He squeezed her tightly to his shoulder as he ran.

When she realized there was no way she could overpower him she wilted in his arms and let him carry her like a sack of potatoes through the streets of the city.

"Are you taking me to my father?"

The man breathed heavily as he ran. "I don't know where he is. I was hoping you could tell me."

"You're the people who took him."

"No, I'm not. I'm a friend of your father. I heard about the explosion at the Council building, but when I got there, your carriage was empty. He told me to find you and your mother should anything happen to him. I figured the explosion, and the empty carriage, meant something happened to him. I haven't found your mother yet, I'm sorry."

"Don't be, she's gone."

He slowed to a jog. "She got away?"

"Not exactly. She's dead."

The man stopped and set Dorothy down. "I'm sorry to hear that, but there's no time to grieve. I have to get you somewhere safe."

He knelt down to her eye level and looked at her. "I am going to take you to some friends of mine. They will take very good care of you while I look for your father."

"I'm going with you."

"It's too dangerous and we don't know where your father is."

"We?"

He glanced left and right and saw that they were alone on the street. "Your father gathered together a small group of people to fight the coming storm."

"He always talked about a storm. What storm?"

He shook his head. "We don't really know, but we think it has something to do with the penal colony."

"I'm coming with you to help find my father."

"You're too young…"

Dorothy yanked herself out of his grip. "Everyone is always saying that. I'm not too young!"

"Dorothy, listen to me. You do not have the training that I have. I can't find and rescue your father if I have to look after you too. Do you trust me?"

Dorothy didn't know why, but she felt she could trust this man, even though she had never met him before in her life. He claimed he was her father's friend, and hadn't acted like the other men who were chasing her. He had even risked his own life to protect her from Ugly.

She was all alone in the world and needed somebody she could trust. He seemed as good a person as any to put her trust in.

"Yes."

"Will you stay with my friends and let them keep you safe?"

"I will on one condition."

"I can't guarantee anything."

Dorothy crossed her arms. "That's not an answer."

"If I can do it I will. That's the best I can offer."

She stared at his face for any hint that he might be lying to her and let the silence hang in the air for a few moments. "Train me to fight like you did back there."

His smile broke into a large grin. "You are much more like your mother than your father."

Dorothy smiled back. "Will you train me?"

He stroked the scruff of a beard forming on his chin. "If you stay with my friends, I will send someone to train you to fight like that."

She stuck out a mud-covered hand. "Deal?"

He regarded her for a moment before grasping her hand in his. "Deal."

She smiled through the dirt and grime on her face. "What is your name?"

He smiled back at her. "William Sipes."

Chapter 3

Dorothy and Edward circled each other inside the barn as they alternated between punching and kicking at each other. He was exactly twice her age, at 30 years old, and nearly a head taller. She did not mind the difference in age and size. The older and bigger they were, the slower they moved, and the harder they fell.

They had been going at each other for so long, they had started to draw a crowd. The younger kids at Uncle Henry and Aunt Em's Farm for Displaced Children gathered around, hollered and cheered as they exchanged blows.

He swung a balled fist at her head. She ducked under his swing and went in to strike at his solar plexus. He quickly deflected her arm and they both hopped back several feet as they continued to circle, bouncing on the balls of their feet like professional boxers in the ring.

Edward smiled. "You're getting faster."

Dorothy brushed away a strand of hair that fell across her face. "I've been practicing."

"And just who have you been practicing with?"

"I've practiced on the cows."

Edward laughed aloud. "I think I'm a little better than a cow."

Dorothy grinned. "Prove it."

"Not going to work Dorothy, you can't goad me into striking first. I practice self-defense, not offense."

She reached in and he batted her hand away.

"Maybe that worked on the cows, but you are going to have to do a lot better than that if you're going to beat me."

He swiped at her and she swatted his hand away just as easily.

They continued to circle as they faced each other across the center of the barn.

More kids finished their chores and joined the small crowd that was growing around them.

Dorothy breathed in time to each step as she hopped from foot to foot and danced around in a circle with Edward.

"When do you go back to London?" she asked as if they were sitting down for tea instead of trying to knock each other to the ground.

"I leave next month for the opening of my academy."

"So, is this my last test?"

"You've either mastered it by now, or you never will."

"If I haven't mastered it by now, maybe it's not a very good fighting style."

"Don't blame my advanced style for your inadequacies. It's going to be a huge hit in England."

Dorothy laughed. "A huge hit," she said putting emphasis on the word hit. "I like that. Have you thought about a name yet?"

"I was thinking of calling it the Academy of Arms and Physical Culture."

"Not your school silly, the name of your fighting style."

"I'm not really sure what to call it. It's a mixture of so many different things all blended together into the perfect form of self-defense."

Dorothy smiled. "Well Mr. Bart, why don't you call it Bart's Jitsu?"

He lowered his arms for a moment. "I told you Dorothy, I don't like being called Mr. Bart."

As if on cue, all the kids gathered around them started chanting, "Mr. Bart, Mr. Bart, Mr. Bart."

He turned his head slightly to admonish the chanting kids and she saw her chance.

She kicked the insole of his left foot, causing him to do the splits and start to fall backward. She grabbed the collar of his shirt and took full advantage of his downward momentum. She swung him around and slammed him face first on to the dirt floor of the barn. She placed both her feet on the back of his knees, yanked his arms behind his back and pulled up on his wrists.

"I would like to submit my final for grading. Let me see if I have the essential principles for Bart's Jitsu correct. Number one; disturb the equilibrium of your assailant. I took advantage of your distraction to knock you off balance.

Check. Number two; surprise him before he has time to regain his balance and use his strength. I threw you down onto the floor of the barn. Check. Number three; subject the joints to strains that they are anatomically and mechanically unable to resist."

She pulled up harder on his wrists and he let out a pained cry. Dorothy smiled. "Check."

Later that night, when the house was completely still and Uncle Henry's snoring lulled the last of the children to sleep, Dorothy stuffed the last of her things into the tiny pack and slung it on her back. She glanced once more at her room to make sure she had not forgotten anything. There wasn't much for a 15-year-old girl to own, so her pack was rather light.

Aunt Em would never let her leave the farm to search for her father if she asked. She practically forced her to sneak out. There were plenty of other kids, other orphans, staying at the farm. She would barely be missed. She tried to keep her promise to William and only ran off a few times during the past five years when she thought she saw her emerald heart glowing. But she hadn't heard from him in over a year and had no other choice but to go out looking again. Every day she spent at the farm, her father's trail grew colder.

So here she was, sneaking out in the middle of the night.

Only this time she knew she was ready.

She had finally bested her teacher that afternoon in the barn and was ready to face whatever obstacles stood between her and her father.

She gritted her teeth with each creak of her bedroom door as it opened slowly. When the door was open just enough for her to slip out, she peeked out into the hallway.

All clear.

She backed out slowly as the door creaked shut.

As soon as she heard the lock click, she spun around and a face emerged from the darkness. Dorothy's heart fluttered and she clamped a hand over her own mouth to keep from yelling out.

The shadows formed into Eloise, another orphaned girl who had been sent to the farm. She was only a couple years older than Dorothy was and would be leaving when she turned eighteen next year.

"What are you doing Dorothy?" Eloise whispered.

"I'm just going to the bathroom." Dorothy whispered back.

Eloise frowned. "With your backpack?"

Dorothy raised her hands, pleading. "Don't tell anyone, Eloise. Please."

"They'll find you again. They always do."

"That's because you always tell them when I leave."

Eloise crossed her arms. "It's not safe out there alone."

"I can take care of myself. Please don't tell anyone this time."

"You know I can't promise that."

"Then at least give me a few hours head start."

Eloise seemed to be waging a battle of her own inside her head. Finally, she let out a big sigh.

"When they notice you don't come down for breakfast I'll say I thought you were going to the bathroom."

Dorothy ran to the window and, with half her body already outside, leaned back. "Thank you Eloise. I won't forget you."

Eloise shrugged. "See you soon."

Dorothy smiled. "Not this time.

Dorothy stood at the front gate by the main road. She looked up one way and then the next.

It would be several hours before the sun came up, but the full moon cast a pallid glow over the long and straight road.

If she went either direction, she would be discovered by anyone who passed by. They would see her walking long before she heard the clatter of horse hooves. She looked across the road to the thickening woods. Traveling through the forest would be slower going, but she could get all the way to town unseen.

She tugged her pack tightly to her back. The woods it was then.

She took one step forward and the ground lit up brightly all around her while she projected a long and dark shadow across the road.

Her heart skipped a beat and she crouched low.

Spinning around, she saw that every one of the recently installed electric lights blazed brightly in the main house.

Eloise had already squealed.

She swore silently under her breath.

She took two steps back away from the road and crawled into the ditch. She had not made it to the safety of the forest, but for the moment, she was out of sight and no longer cast a tell-tale shadow.

She hazarded a peek. Uncle Henry was standing on the porch slowly scanning the road in both directions.

Good. He hadn't seen her yet. Aunt Em tugged her robe tightly around her body to ward off the chilly air as she joined him on the porch. She was too far away to hear what they said but when Uncle Henry pointed to the barn Dorothy swore again, this time using stronger words.

She had to get into the forest and through the creek if she had any hope of getting away tonight.

She peeked up again to see Uncle Henry heading for the barn. If she didn't run now, she would never make it to the creek in time.

She pointed herself back to the road, crouched like one of the barn cats stalking a mouse and took three deep breaths to force oxygen into her blood. She was going to need every ounce of strength she could muster if she planned to outrun what was coming after her.

She sprang up from the ditch and ran full speed across the road and into the woods.

She could just make out Aunt Em shouting for her to stop.

She ran full speed for nearly ten minutes through the forest. Her lungs burned, her muscles ached, and her feet tripped over the unsteady ground more often than not.

She leaned against a tree and tried to listen to the forest around her.

It was nearly impossible to hear anything except her pounding heart and gasping breath. She stifled a cough and shut her eyes.

She reminded herself why she was even out here. She thought of happier times with her mother and father and let a smile play on the corners of her lips. Her heart quieted down and her breathing slowed.

For a moment, the silence of the forest greeted her.

A slight breeze rustled the leaves above her. It cooled her overheated face.

But the soft breeze did not bring only relief. The cool night air also carried the sounds of Uncle Henry's dogs as they yelped their excitement for another chance at hunting her.

Her body begged her to sit down and wait for capture.

She couldn't do that.

Mind over body. That's what her father always said. Probably because he was more of a scientist then he was an athlete.

Her mind forced her body to obey as she pushed off from the tree that kept her from falling over from exhaustion. She realized she was still half a kilometer away from the creek. She had to do something to get the dogs off her trail. The creek would have worked, but she would never reach it before they surrounded her.

She didn't think they would kill her. Uncle Henry would never allow it, and they only did what he allowed. But being bitten was not fun, either.

She had to slow them down.

Her father's voice sprang into her head again.

Mind over body.

Right, Father, she thought back. I'm forcing my body to keep moving even though it wants to stop.

Her father's voice sounded even more insistent.

Mind over body.

What was he trying to say to her?

Mind over body.

She stopped and listened. The dogs were closer. They were faster than she could ever be.

Mind over body.

"I heard you the first time," she said aloud.

She jumped at the sound of her own voice. But it was in that moment she knew what she needed to do.

She could never outrun them. But she could outsmart them.

Mind over body.

A plan immediately formed in her mind. "Thanks Dad," she said aloud.

She looked around her at the forest. She scanned every tree looking for the one that would serve her purpose.

She stopped at one. This tree was perfect.

The barking was getting louder. Whatever she had to do, she had to do it quickly.

She circled the tree several times, dragging her backpack on the ground around it. Slinging her pack over her shoulder, she began the harsh climb up the tree.

The dogs would easily find her.

Uncle Henry stopped every minute and listened. The dogs yipped rapidly. The trail was getting fresher the closer they got to her and they were getting more excited.

He silently cursed Dorothy for her stubborn refusal to accept the truth. A truth that solidified for every year that passed.

There had been no ransom. No indication from anybody that Dorothy's father was alive.

She insisted that he was out there somewhere and that, despite the best efforts of the New

Kansas police, a little girl could strike out on her own and find him when they couldn't.

She had to face reality.

Her father was not out there to be found.

Maybe it was time to put a lock on her door so they could all start getting a full night's sleep.

He stopped again and listened. The yelping was closer and sporadic. They had stopped their pursuit. And since they were not near the creek, it could mean only one thing.

They had found her.

Uncle Henry increased his pace and caught up with the dogs as they were taking turns leaping at the base of a tree. They stopped as soon as he arrived and all sat down in strict obedience. Half of them looked up at the tree while the other half looked to him for instructions.

He twisted the focal lens on his lamp and shone it up the tree. Dorothy's backpack reflected back his light.

"I know you're up there Dorothy. Come on down."

Dorothy gripped the tree to keep herself from falling. Her dry tongue scraped across her chapped lips. Her muscles screamed for relief. Climbing the tree had sapped nearly all her remaining strength.

It had been much harder than running through the forest.

She had stopped sweating, nearly all the excess water in her body depleted.

The only water she had brought with her was in her backpack in the tree across the creek.

She hoped she had jumped far enough that there was a break between her scent around the tree and the new path she carved toward the creek.

Dorothy let go of the trunk of the tree she leaned on and tested a little bit of weight on her ankle.

She winced from the pain caused by landing wrong on her foot. Mind over body, she reminded herself.

A smiled formed as she thought about Uncle Henry, who was probably only now figuring out she was not up the tree.

The sun was just peeking over the mountains by the time she made it to the edge of town. She had intended to be through this town and halfway to the next by sunrise. Her ankle was starting to feel better, but it still slowed her down.

She decided to enter town from one of the side alleys rather than the main road. She didn't want to attract too much attention since news of her previous escape attempts had spread like wildfire in a small town were very little ever happened.

It would not do to have nosy town-folk alert Uncle Henry or Aunt Em where she was before she even started looking for her father. As she slipped into the alley from one of the farms that lined the town along the eastern edge, she saw a group of men all gathered around someone who cowered before them against the wall of the alleyway.

As she got closer, she could hear the men taunting the boy at their feet.

"What are you going to do about it freak boy?"

The boy at their feet, hidden by his cloak and large cowl hood, looked at the feet of his assailants. "I do not wish to do anything."

Another one of the men kicked him. "That's right; you just lay there like a frightened little kitten."

Dorothy forgot all about her twisted ankle and hollered down the alley. "You leave him alone."

In unison, the four men all turned to look at her. The biggest of the four, obviously the leader, stared hard at her. "This ain't no business of yours."

"If you're picking on one of my friends, it is my business."

The leader smiled, showing her his tobacco stained teeth. "I'm pretty sure this ain't no friend of yours."

"And how do you know that?"

The leader leaned down and yanked the cowl hood off the boy and Dorothy's eyes widened in surprise.

The first thing she noticed was that his head was covered in a golden fur. Not hair, but animal-like fur. He lifted his head to look at her and his face was almost cat-like in appearance. The bright sunlight cutting in over the farms and shining into the alley forced his pupils to contract. But they didn't contract into pinpoint dots. Instead, they thinned into slits just like the barn cats' eyes did back at the farm.

The last thing she noticed was the complete and utter lack of fear in his eyes. He didn't seem to be afraid of these men, but everything else about his mannerisms, and what he said, was to make them think he was afraid.

She didn't know why he was acting like a coward in front of these men, but there was no way she was going to pretend that they frightened her.

She quickly composed herself and looked back at the leader with a smile. "Of course that's my friend."

The leader started walking toward her. "I guess if you plan to stand up for the little freak, you should be put into your place just like him."

The other three joined in behind him as they all started toward her, completely ignoring the half-boy half-cat creature in favor of someone who was willing to give them a fight. And each one of them, judging by the scars on their faces and clenched fists, enjoyed a good fight.

Or more likely, she thought, since each of them alone was three times her size, they were someone who enjoyed picking on people much smaller than they were.

She hated bullies.

Especially bullies who were bigger than she was. Then again, the bigger they were, the harder they fell.

Despite the bravado in her voice and her defiantly upraised chin, her heart thundered deep inside her chest.

The only other person she had ever fought with in hand-to-hand combat was Edward. It had been obvious from the start that he always pulled his punches and held back whenever they sparred. He had never wanted to hurt her.

These men bearing down on her in the alley had nothing but murder in their eyes. It was obvious they wanted to do her great bodily harm just for interrupting them from doing great bodily harm to someone else.

Events slowed to a crawl around her as her mind raced to assess the situation and apply the principles that Edward had taught her. In addition, practicing on cows was about to pay off because that prepared her for dealing with the sheer weight of each of the men coming at her.

Edward's training tips flipped through her mind until she settled on the one that made the most sense for dealing with the men getting closer. Any fighting force always put their strongest man up front to both intimidate and weaken the enemy during first contact.

Dorothy shifted her focus to the fourth man, who positioned himself at the rear of the group. Still more than twice her size, he was decidedly the weakest of the four.

That settled it.

The first thing she had to do was thin the herd and generate a little intimidation of her own.

It would not help her to stand there and wait until the men reached her. She needed to build a little kinetic energy of her own.

So she rushed at them.

The leader half crouched with an evil grin on his face. He was obviously enjoying her making the first move.

She ducked under his swing and darted past him. She ran across the alley diagonally and then hopped up and took two steps along the wall, which propelled her past the next two men.

She launched herself off the wall and came straight down onto the last man. This caught him utterly by surprise as she aimed her elbow right for the bridge of his nose. His nose flattened in an instant and became a crimson river as he stumbled backward and crumpled to the ground. Dorothy snatched one of his arms, stuck it between her legs and twisted it until she heard the satisfying crack of bones breaking.

One down three to go, she thought to herself as she crouched ready for the next attack.

The remaining three men spun around and looked at their friend lying unconscious at her feet, his face covered in his own blood.

The leader sneered at her. "You got lucky, little girl."

She sneered back. "I can take you all together or one at a time. Your choice."

Two of the men simultaneously rushed her, each gripping a dagger in their hand.

When fighting multiple assailants, the tactics she used had to change. She darted toward them, causing them to spread out so they would not stab each other when they slashed at her.

She leaped in the air and kicked one in the face while the other slashed at her with his dagger. The first man fell backward from her boot in his face, leaving her to only worry about the one trying to gut her at the moment. Once the dagger swept past her, she grabbed the arm and twisted it as she fell back down to the ground, pulling him down with her. Before her feet touched the ground, she heard the snapping sound. The man cried out in pain and his dagger clattered noisily to the ground. She kicked him sideways and he slammed into the wall and fell to the ground without moving again.

She spun around ready to defend herself against the man she kicked in the face, but saw that when he went down his head had collided with a barrel and he lay unconscious.

She heard the faint sound of wind whistling and ducked just before the leader's dagger sliced her throat.

He tossed the dagger back and forth from hand-to-hand. "You are pretty feisty for a girl. I am going to enjoy our time together."

He was incredibly fast for someone so big. He continued to slash at her, cutting her coat into ribbons as she ducked and dodged.

She punched and kicked him repeatedly, but he never reacted.

She started backing up as he continued to slash at her with his dagger.

He was keeping her off balance. It was step number two in Edward's self-defense essentials.

And she was on the receiving end of it.

He smiled at her with an evil grin because he knew he had gained the advantage. He swung the dagger wide and, as her eyes tracked it, he punched her on the side of her head with his other hand.

She went down hard but used the momentum to roll back up to her feet. Her ears rang from the blow to her head and, just as she focused on her attacker, he hit her with another two punches and a solid kick to her stomach.

She sprawled backward from the impact and landed on her back in the middle of the alley.

He towered over her and gripped the dagger tightly in his hand. He knelt on her chest and held the dagger up against her cheek. He still wore that evil grin as he looked down at her. "This has been fun. But I can think of something you and I can do that is much more fun."

He slid the dagger down and tucked the blade under her coat. She tried to struggle but all he did was apply more pressure with his knee and forced the wind out of her.

He pulled up on the dagger and she heard the front of her coat being torn open. She had never seen this kind of look in a man's eyes before and she was terrified.

He started to apply all his weight on her chest, choking the last remaining breath out of her, when he suddenly roared out in pain. He released his grip on the dagger and clawed at something on his back. He fell sideways and, with his knee gone, she sucked hungrily at the air as she rolled to one side to get away from him.

When her body no longer demanded oxygen, she forced her eyes to focus on the writhing shapes before her. The man had torn the boy off his back and was now slamming him repeatedly against the wall.

She snatched the dagger from the ground in front of her and rammed it into the back of the large man. He bellowed out in a rage before collapsing at her feet in an expanding pool of his own blood.

She took two steps and then collapsed to the ground herself. The boy was immediately at her side and lifted her up into his arms. "Let's get you home."

Henry slammed his fist onto the dining room table. "You can't do that!"

Emma flinched and reached to steady the salt shaker that teetered in the center of the table from the impact. She glanced over to Ms. Butterfield, who didn't seem the least bit phased by his outburst.

Instead, she sat quietly with her hands folded in her lap. Even her voice stayed calm when she spoke, as if she knew she held all the power. Which she did.

"I can and I will."

And she would, thought Emma.

Emma placed a hand on Henry's arm and looked into Ms. Butterfield's eyes for any hint of sympathy.

"She's family."

Ms. Butterfield's eyes were cold and dark. There would be no sympathy from her.

"She's not blood family. I have several witnesses that say she attacked a group of men in town."

Henry laughed out loud. "A 15-year-old girl attacked a group of men all by herself, without provocation, beat them up and walked away without a scratch?"

"I visited the victims myself in the hospital. A couple of them had broken bones, one of them was still unconscious, and another looked like he had been bitten on the neck and stabbed in the back. It was a very savage attack."

Henry's face portrayed a mixture of amusement and shock. "Are you even listening to what you're saying?"

"If you can't control her, it is my responsibility to…"

He cut her off. "If any of this is true, then why are you here and not the police?"

Ms. Butterfield sat up a little straighter in her chair. "They refuse to press any charges."

Henry leaned back in his own chair with a tiny smirk. "I wonder why that is?"

The front door opened and they all turned at once to see who it was.

Emma was the first to jump up. "Oh my God, Dorothy!"

She was a horrific sight. Her clothes torn, her face covered in grime and streaked with tears. She leaned heavily on an old tree branch as she hobbled in through the doorway, favoring her left leg. She was not the same girl who left twelve hours earlier.

Emma rushed over and hugged her tightly. Dorothy mumbled something into her shoulder.

She pulled back. "What?"

"I'm sorry Aunt Em. I promise I won't try to run away again."

Emma smiled, tears rolling down her cheeks. "It's okay honey. We just want you safe."

Henry snapped his head from Dorothy to Ms. Butterfield. "I hardly think that anyone in that condition could have done even half of what these men claim."

Ms. Butterfield cleared her throat. Emma turned around to see her looking down her nose at them. "If she should run away again, I will have no choice but to place her into a new home."

Ms. Butterfield gathered her small bag and strode past them and out the door without so much as a goodbye.

Henry dropped down to Dorothy's eye level.

"Did you hear what she said?"

Dorothy nodded her head. "I promise. From now on, I will be the best kid you have here."

Emma smiled. "You were always the best. But don't tell any of the rest of them I said that."

Despite the pain she was obviously experiencing, Dorothy let out a small laugh.

Chapter 4

William Sipes was roused from a deep sleep by the alarm bell of his nickel-plated Ansonia 'Peep O Day' carriage clock. He smacked a sleepy hand around to the back of the carriage clock and reset the alarm lever.

He tossed the comforter over the edge of the bed. He sat up yawning and stretching as he swung his feet over the edge to the cold hardwood floor. He scratched in all the inappropriate places as he headed out of the sparsely furnished bedroom and down the hall to the parlor room.

The parlor room looked more like a mad scientist's laboratory than a room where Victorian society gathered at night to play games and converse about politics. Various pieces of electronic equipment were scattered about the room in a seemingly haphazard layout. Every piece of equipment was connected by wires to every other piece of equipment and there was a constant buzzing sound emanating from the largest contraptions.

All of this equipment was wired to the focal point of the parlor room, a specially designed Tesla oscillator capable of detecting the faintest wireless electronic transmission from halfway around the world.

There were three such specially designed Tesla oscillators in the entire world. The first one was in the Americas, the second was in Eastern Europe and the last one was right here, in New Kansas. Together, they covered nearly 80% of the civilized world. They were designed to listen for one signal and one signal alone.

He stepped into the parlor and froze. Leaning back in the chair in front of the Tesla oscillator in New Kansas was Reginald. His sole job for the past six hours was to listen for that signal. But instead of doing that, he was asleep.

William kicked the legs of the chair and it collapsed backward. Reginald was awake before he hit the ground.

Reginald rolled to his hands and knees and looked up at him. "What'd you do that for?"

William reached down, grabbed him by the lapels of his coat and hauled him to his feet. "Do you think what we're doing is a game?"

Reginald shook himself out of William's grip. "I don't know what your problem is…"

"My problem?" He shook his head and barked out a laugh. "My problem is that you don't take this job seriously enough."

"Not serious enough?" Reginald pointed to the large speaker that emitted a faint hiss. "We have been listening to that radio frequency 24 hours a day for seven years. And do you know what we've heard in all that time? Nothing."

"Do you want to be the one to tell a 17-year-old girl the only reason we never heard from her father is that we were asleep at the wheel when something finally came through?

"We'll never have to say that."

"And what makes you think that?"

Reginald shook his head. "Nothing's happening William. Nothing ever has and nothing ever will."

"You don't know that."

"Yes I do. We all do."

"Then what are you doing here?"

Reginald smoothed the lapels of his coat. "If you haven't noticed, we're in the middle of a great recession. Jobs are hard to come by since the panic of '93. I'll take anything that pays, even if it's on the other side of the world."

"Pack your stuff and get out."

Reginald smiled. "Don't be like that William; it won't happen again I swear."

William stared hard at him. "You're right. It won't."

"William I…"

"Maybe you do not understand me. You're fired Reggie."

"You can't fire me. I'm the only one who knows how to tune this thing when the frequency creeps out of alignment."

"We can find someone else who will treat this with the seriousness it deserves."

"You know what? This was a stupid job anyway. Sitting here six hours a day and listening to that speaker do nothing but… "

The speaker crackled to life and a faint voice could barely be heard. William lifted the chair back to a sitting position and sat down in it. He twisted the dial trying to get the voice to come in more clearly. The speaker responded with a squelch and the voice faded away.

Reginald hovered over his shoulder. "You're turning it the wrong way."

He turned to face Reginald. "Didn't I fire you?"

Reginald looked at him with a half-smile. "That was before anything happened. Now you need me."

He put a hand on William's shoulder. "I can get that voice to come in loud and clear. If you want to hear what Professor Gale has to say, you better let me back into that chair."

He moved out of the chair and watched as Reginald's expert hands twisted the dial and the voice became clear.

"… in OZ…"

He leaned into the speaker and turned to Reginald. "It's cutting in and out. Can you get the complete signal?"

Reginald was furiously flipping switches and twisting dials. "What do you think I'm doing?"

He twisted the dial some more and the speaker came back to life. "… bring the emerald…"

"It cut out again!"

"I'm working as fast as I can." Reginald twisted the dial slowly trying to focus on the signal. "… spin it… find me…"

The voice stopped and there was nothing but static coming from the speaker. Reginald flipped a few more switches and spun the dial. Nothing but static came out of the speaker. For five minutes Reginald continued to flip switches and turn dials until he finally sat back in his chair. "I'm sorry William, he's not transmitting anymore."

William stared at the wall, lost in thought. His head spun with the possibility that, after all this time, they would finally find Professor Gale. He had prepared for this moment and he was ready. He was practically bouncing up and down on his feet in anticipation for the rescue of his old friend.

He looked at Reginald. "Alert the strike team. We leave before dawn."

Reginald gave him a quizzical look. "Whoa, slow down. Where are we going exactly?"

"You heard the Professor. He's in OZ."

"You can't take the strike team in there. It's a prison. We'll be killed."

"If that's where Professor Gale is, then that's where I'm going."

"Do you know how big the penal colony is? How do you expect to find him there based on a couple of garbled words?"

"He said all we had to do was spin the emerald to find him."

"I didn't hear that."

He clapped Reginald on the shoulder and smiled. It was the first truly happy smile he'd had in the past seven years. "Well that's what I heard."

Chapter 5

A hand clamped over Dorothy's mouth. It stifled her scream as she became instantly awake.

She felt the breath of someone moving to whisper in her ear in the darkness.

"Shh, Dorothy, it's William."

He released her mouth and flipped the switch on the portable lamp by the side of her bed. The soft warm glow of the incandescent bulb made him look years younger than he was. Her heart began to thump harder. There was only one reason he would be here.

"You found my father!"

"Keep your voice down."

"But you found him right?"

"Not yet. We heard from him and he told me something I need to verify. Do you have the emerald he gave you?"

It had taken her a couple of years to save up enough money to buy a necklace and have the emerald heart mounted in it. Ever since that day, she kept her father's emerald heart next to her own heart.

She slipped it out from under her shirt. "Always."

He smiled and held out his hand. "Let me see it for a moment."

She slipped the necklace over her head and handed it to him. She watched as he popped the emerald heart out of the necklace and looked around the room.

Curiosity was getting the better of her. "What are you looking for?"

He glanced at her. "I need a small piece of glass. Anything smooth that I can lay down flat."

She pointed toward her dresser. "What about my hand mirror?"

He smiled. "Perfect."

He placed the emerald onto the surface of the mirror. He looked hesitantly at her and then gripped the emerald with his thumb and forefinger and spun it.

She walked over and looked down at it spinning. "What are you doing?" she whispered.

"Testing a theory," he whispered back.

She watched as the emerald spun effortlessly on the smooth mirror until it slowed and came to an abrupt stop. William looked in the direction that the point of the heart was facing and then glanced out the window to get his bearings.

He smiled and then spun the emerald again, this time even faster.

She watched again as the emerald slowed and stopped abruptly, pointing in the same direction it had before.

He smiled bigger. "Now you spin it."

Dorothy gripped the emerald between her thumb and forefinger and spun it. Her finger slipped and the emerald wobbled without spinning very quickly.

"Whoops," she said as she reached for it to spin it again.

William grabbed her wrist. "No, let it go."

It wobbled unsteadily for a couple of revolutions before it wobbled to a stop. William's grin threatened to spread to his ears.

It was pointing in the exact same direction it had pointed the last two times they spun it.

She stared at the emerald, her mind trying to deny what she had seen.

It couldn't be, could it?

She looked up and searched William's eyes for the truth.

He nodded his head and smiled. "It's pointing to your father."

He grabbed the emerald and popped it back into the necklace casing.

He gripped her shoulders and smiled. "We've listened to a specific wireless channel for the last seven years. Your father finally got a message out to us. He is in the Outcast Zone and told me that if we spun the emerald it would point to him."

She fought back the tears that glisten in the corners of her eyes. "What did he say? Is he okay?"

"The message cut out abruptly and we barely got the information that we did. I don't know how he is doing or where he is, but I will find him and bring him back."

Dorothy swallowed the lump in her throat and felt her heart race. The ability to find her father had been with her the whole time. Why hadn't he told her?

She remembered how quickly the events took place when the men took him. It happened so fast he never had a chance.

She immediately opened the dresser drawer and started pulling out clothing.

William looked at her with a sideways glance. "What are you doing?"

She continued to grab clothing out of the drawer without looking at him. "I'm coming with you."

He shook his head. "No Dorothy, it's too dangerous."

She spun to face him, the rage welling up inside of her. "Don't tell me I'm too young to do this. I'm not that little girl you first met covered in mud and tears. I know how to fight just as well as you do. Hell, I might even be better than you."

"You watch your language young lady."

"Don't change the subject. I'm going."

"No you're not!"

She moved in close and pointed a finger at his face. "You can't tell me…"

He batted her hand out of his face. "I'm not discussing this."

"What's going on in here?"

They both jumped at the sound of someone else in the room and turned to see Eloise standing in the open doorway.

William slipped the emerald necklace into his pocket. "Nothing. I was just leaving."

Dorothy vaulted the bed and stood between him and the door. "Not without me you're not."

Eloise looked back and forth at them. "What's going on Dorothy? Who is he?"

William smiled at Eloise. "I'm an old friend of Dorothy's father. I just came to get something I needed."

Dorothy sidestepped to stay in his way as he tried to go around her. "And you need me."

He grabbed her shoulders and pushed her to the side. "Where I am going is far too dangerous for you. Stay here and I will bring your father back. I promise."

He walked out the door with her emerald necklace, the only thing she could use to find her father.

Chapter 6

Dorothy counted to ten before she grabbed her backpack and shoved clothes into it.

Eloise stood in the doorway and stared at her. "What are you doing Dorothy?"

She stopped, went over to Eloise and placed her hands on her shoulders.

"Promise me you won't tell Uncle Henry or Aunt Em I left until morning."

Eloise shook her head. "I…"

Dorothy gripped her shoulders harder. "I have to find my father and following that man is the only way I can do it. I have to leave now before he gets too far."

She returned to shoving only the essentials into her backpack.

Eloise followed her out into the hallway.

"Are you ever coming back?"

Dorothy smiled. "If I find my father, I won't need to come back."

Eloise looked like she was ready to cry. "I'll miss you."

Dorothy gave her a big hug. "I'll miss you too."

Dorothy hopped out the window and landed on the ground in a crouch. She ran up to the corner of the house and peeked around it. William was warming up his French built steam car called La Rapide because it could reach speeds of up to sixty-two kilometers per hour.

Any hope she had of following him on foot immediately melted away. At speeds like that, she would need a horse to be able to keep up with him. But not just any horse, she would need a fast one. And none of Uncle Henry's old cart-pulling mares were young enough. Or fast enough.

William was focused on bringing the boiler to enough pressure so that he could drive off. He would never agree to let her come along, so she had to sneak on board that car. She could see steam escaping from the release valve. He was almost ready to leave.

Fortunately for her, a cloud swept in front of the moon and it fell dark all around the farm. She used the cover of darkness to run across the field and leaned up against the side of the barn. William would have to pass right by this barn to get to the road that paralleled the farm.

She tightened the shoulder straps on her backpack and jogged softly in place to warm up her leg muscles.

The cloud passed and moonlight once again brightened the farm. It did not matter, she reminded herself. She would be behind him when she made a run for it.

William would never see her and, the road was so rough, he would never feel her jump on the back of the steam car. And then she would be one step closer to finding her father.

Almost too easy, she thought and let a smile tease the corners of her mouth.

She watched as William disengaged the brake and pushed on the lever that would drive power from the steam engine to the wheels.

She took three quick breaths and readied herself to run behind the accelerating steam car and jump on the back.

She turned away quickly and knelt down beside the barn to stay in shadow as every light in the house blazed brightly in an instant.

"Eloise," she said under her breath. Why didn't she leave when she turned 18? Because then she could not stick around and cause trouble for Dorothy.

William stopped the steam car before he even got halfway to the barn and looked back at the brightly lit house.

Uncle Henry came out the front door and waved to William.

William hopped down out of the steam car and jogged back to the front of house.

She was too far to hear anything over the chugging sound of the steam car, but she knew that Uncle Henry was telling William what Eloise had told him. They both glanced around the brightly lit farm. William shook Uncle Henry's hand and trotted back to the steam car.

Uncle Henry stayed on the porch and continued to look back and forth.

There was no way she was going to be able to run out and jump onto the steam car now. Uncle Henry would spot her immediately.

She crawled around the back of the barn and noticed the barn's shadow stretched all the way to the road. She knew if she could make it to the road, she could get up behind the steam car and jump on to it. But the road was a lot smoother and William would be driving a lot faster.

It wasn't a great idea, but it was the only idea she had left.

As she crouched and ran along the shadow of the barn, doubt crept into her thoughts.

What if William turned and went the other way down the road?

What if he was going too fast?

She pushed those negative thoughts deep down and reminded herself that this was all about finding her father. She would outrun a thoroughbred racehorse if she had too.

She reached the road and looked down just as William turned on to the main road. His carriage lamps swept across the forest she had run through the last time she made an escape attempt and then pointed down the road at her.

Good news. He was headed her way.

She crouched down in the ditch so the carriage lamps would not give her away before he passed her.

She squinted her eyes against the brightening light of the carriage lamps and felt the rush of wind as the steam car swept by.

She leaped out of the ditch and ran full speed down the middle of the road toward the back of the steam car.

She ran as fast as she could and was gaining on the car. There was a loud puff of steam and the car shot forward.

She started to lose ground.

The car was getting further away.

Fear engulfed her. If she didn't catch up to that car, she would never be able to follow William to her father.

She struggled with the weight of the backpack and realized it was slowing her down.

She stripped off the backpack and surged faster.

It was no use; the car was speeding up and leaving her farther behind.

Another loud puff of steam and the car suddenly slowed to a crawl.

She forced her muscles to run faster. She caught up to the steam car and grabbed the back railing when another loud puff of steam propelled the car forward, dragging her off her feet.

She clung to the railing and scrambled to get her feet off the ground before the tops of her shoes were torn to shreds.

She wedged her feet into a crevice along the bottom edge of the steam car and held on for dear life as they sped through the town and turned onto the road that led to the airfield.

Chapter 7

Dorothy let go of the rail handhold and dropped from the steam car just as William turned onto the airfield. She rolled into a ball and tumbled unceremoniously off the edge of the road and into the ditch. She sat up and carefully moved her arms and legs before twisting her head back and forth.

Whew! Nothing was broken or too badly bruised. While she tested the rest of her body for damage, she wondered what she'd ever done in her life to keep ending up in the ditch like this. Hopefully, she mused, this was the last time she would have to spiral out of control to the ground.

She scrambled to her feet and ran along the fence that bordered the airfield.

Her target was the only airship that was brightly lit up. That had to be the one William was preparing for departure. If she could sneak on board and hide, maybe they wouldn't discover her until well past the point of no return. William would have no choice but to let her come along. She could fight. She could think on her feet. William would realize that having her along was better than leaving her behind.

As she got closer, she saw several men loading large wooden crates into the rear cargo area of the gondola mounted to the underside of the airship envelope. Some of the crates were so big they looked like they could hold an adult man with plenty of room to spare. They looked like a poor man's coffin.

She wondered what was in the large crates but did not have to wonder long. Two men dropped one of the crates while they were carrying it up the ramp. It landed sideways and the lid broke off. Several rifles spilled out of the crate and to the ground.

The man who had been supervising the rest as they loaded the crates hollered out. "What are you, a couple of parlor soldiers? Be careful with those things."

One of the men hollered back. "Don't worry Sarge, these are Spencer carbines. We could drag these barkers through the mud and they'd still fire twenty rounds per minute."

The second man pointed to the first. "Blame the Jonah here; I had a good grip on my end."

The first man turned on the second. "I ain't no bad luck!"

Sarge had obviously heard enough. "Get back to work and hide those rifles before someone sees them."

The two men scrambled to put the rifles back into the crate and replaced the lid, but Sarge was not done with them yet. "And as soon as you finish loading that crate get the rest of them in the airship now."

Dorothy scanned the area around the airship and, in just that moment, it seemed everyone was facing away from her.

This was her chance to sneak on board.

She ran to the remaining stack of crates waiting to be loaded. There were too many people around for her to make the last 40 meter run to the loading ramp and up into the airship. She had to find another way inside.

The two men, who had dropped the earlier crate, walked back down the loading ramp and headed for the stack of crates that was her hiding spot.

She was trapped.

If she ran back to the fence, they would see her. But she couldn't stay hiding behind the crates; they would see her as soon as they picked up the first crate.

She placed her hand on top of the crate next to her to steady herself and use it as a launching point to dash across the field. The lid shifted slightly as soon as she touched it. She slipped her thumb under the lip of the lid and lifted it up.

She peaked inside and saw more rifles nestled among the straw packing. There was just enough room for her inside and, just as the two men approached, she lowered the lid on top of her.

Their voices were only slightly muffled by the crudely built wooden crate.

"With all these guns, you'd think we were launching an invasion."

"To hear William talk, we pretty much are."

"Then let's get these barkers loaded before we're left out of the fun."

Dorothy stomach flip-flopped as the men lifted the crate she was in.

"I swear, each crate feels heavier than the last."

"Whoa hold on. The lid is loose on this crate. I don't want a repeat of last time when you drop this one too."

"I'm not the one who dropped it! You are!"

They set the crate down with a heavy thump, the rifles jumping and jabbing her all over.

"Hand me those nails."

She covered her ears against the loud pounding as they nailed the lid shut on her coffin-like crate.

"There, now you can drop it all you want."

The other man grumbled and mumbled some choice words under his breath as they carried the crate up the ramp and into the gondola.

She laid there quietly for over an hour as they finished loading the gondola. Every time she heard them shuffling up the ramp with another crate, she prayed that they would not stack it on top of hers.

They never did and when she heard them locking the cargo bay doors, she knew she had made it.

It was another half hour before her stomach alerted her that the airship had launched and was airborne.

During a quiet moment, she strained to listen if there was anybody in the cargo area.

She couldn't hear anything and she got the sense that she was alone. She pushed up with her hands and feet against the lid.

The wood flexed under her pressure but the nails held fast.

She rolled over to her stomach and tried to force the lid off by pushing up into a kneeling position and muscling her back and shoulders into the top of the crate.

They had used way more nails than they needed to, and the lid was not budging even a little.

She rolled back over, fatigued from all of her exerted, but ultimately useless, effort.

She was trapped with nothing to do but wait to be discovered.

It was hard for her to stay awake, locked in the dark crate and cradled by straw. She was exhausted and found herself dozing off, occasionally waking to voices in the cargo area before falling asleep again.

Dorothy jerked out of a deep slumber by the sound of rough-hewn nails being forced from the lid of her crate. The crate lid lifted up and she found herself staring into William's face.

He did not look happy.

"There you are."

He reached a hand down and pulled her out of the crate.

"Someone mentioned they thought they saw a girl hiding among the crates back at the airfield. I knew it had to be you."

She looked around and saw the lids were pried off from nearly every crate in the cargo area. She looked back at him and gave him a sheepish grin.

That did not change the look on his face one bit.

He grabbed her by the arm and hauled her into the passenger compartment of the gondola and tossed her down on one of the overstuffed chairs bolted to the floor.

"What were you thinking, Dorothy."

"I want to help you find my father."

He shook his head. "You've put me in an awful position. Where we are going is far too dangerous for you and we don't have time to turn back now."

"I can help."

"My job is to keep you safe and I can't do that if you fight me every step of the way."

She looked away from him and out the window. It was then she realized her mistake.

He touched her chin with the tip of his finger and twisted her head away from the window to face him. "What do you have to say for yourself?"

"I should have snuck aboard the other airship."

His eyebrows furrowed. "What other airship?"

She pointed out the window at the airship flying alongside them.

At the same moment he looked, the side of the other airship was suddenly engulfed in black smoke accompanied by the thunderous boom of cannon fire.

William roared, "Get down!"

He tackled her to the floor and covered her body with his in the same moment the sides of the gondola exploded inward.

A second thunderous explosion sent cannonballs into the envelope above the gondola that kept the airship in the air.

The entire airship began to roll to one side from the impact.

She pushed up on William and tried to force him off of her. But he must have been unconscious and was a dead weight.

The airship continue to roll to one side and William finally rolled off of her and continued to roll until he wedged against the wall of the gondola that was now the floor. She got on her hands and knees and shuffled over to him. His final unselfish act of shielding her with his body had saved her life, but ended his. His body shifted again as the airship continued to tilt. She did not have time to mourn his death.

She groped through his coat pockets and her hand gripped the hard object inside tightly as she let out the breath she had been holding.

She wiped William's blood off the emerald necklace and slipped it back into her own pocket where it belonged.

The airship tilted wildly as it continued to spin out of control.

Men were running around as cannon balls continued to rip through the passenger compartment of the gondola.

The other airship was now only firing as fast as each cannon could reload, so each shot was more sporadic and less destructive than the initial volley had been.

Her airship spun in a half circle and she stood on the roof of the gondola. She looked at the chairs still bolted to what, from her perspective, was now the ceiling.

The airship continued to rotate on its central axis and soon the big gaping hole on the side of the gondola would become the floor. If she stayed here she would fall out, and she could tell by the slight bend to the horizon they were still hundreds, if not thousands, of meters above the ground.

She had to think of something and had to think of it quick.

Many of William's men were killed during the first attack. Those who survived soon fell screaming through the holes ripped out of the walls of the gondola.

A few of them had managed to retrieve rifles from the cargo area and were now firing back at the other airship.

They clung to chairs and railings as they tried to keep from falling out of the airship.

A hand grabbed Dorothy's ankle. She screamed and looked at who had grabbed her. Her fear turned to instant relief. "William!"

He struggled to his feet in the still spinning airship.

Blood seeped from his mouth as he spoke. "I have to keep you safe."

He pushed Dorothy ahead of him, through the door, and back into the cargo area.

Every crate had spilled its contents when the airship rolled upside down.

William grabbed the nearest large crate and shoveled handfuls of straw into it. When it was filled nearly three quarters of the way full, he turned to Dorothy. "Get in!"

Dorothy shook her head. "No way."

He grabbed her, shoved her into the crate and slammed the lid shut. The hammering of nails into the lid drowned out her cries for him to stop.

When he finished, he put his mouth against one of the crevices. "Bury yourself into the middle of the straw and…"

A massive explosion cut him off and Dorothy tumbled inside the crate as the airship tumbled out of control toward the ground.

The Adventure Continues...

Other Books by the Author

A is for Apprentice (Fantasy)

Oliver Twist: Victorian Vampire (Fantasy)

A Tale of Two Cities with Dragons (Fantasy)

Shade Infinity (Science Fiction Thriller)

Peacekeepers X-Alpha Series (Thriller)
> Inherit the Throne
> The Warrior's Code

Steampunk OZ Series (Science Fiction Serial)
> Forgotten Girl
> The Legacy's World
> Emerald Shadow
> The Future's Destiny

The Dangerous Captive

Missing Legacy

Shadow of History

The Edge of the Hunter

Fugue: The Cure (Science Fiction Short Story)

Stay informed about all the trouble I keep getting into. Subscribe to Steve DeWinter's Book Report (i.e. the mailing list) @ SteveDW.com